22/1.....

D0186690

GUINEA PIG PARTY

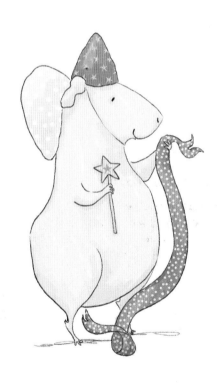

H46 642 824 9

For Honey and all her little friends
who inspired this book xxx

Nosy Crow Ltd
The Crow's Nest,
10a Lant Street,
London SE1 1QR
www.nosycrow.com

First published in hardback 2012
This edition published 2013
ISBN 978 0 85763 086 5 (HB)
ISBN 978 0 85763 088 9 (PB)

Nosy Crow and associated logos are trademarks
and/or registered trademarks of Nosy Crow Ltd.

Text and illustrations copyright © Holly Surplice 2012

The right of Holly Surplice to be identified as the author
and illustrator of this work has been asserted.

All rights reserved

This book is sold subject to the condition that it shall not, by way of trade or otherwise, be lent,
hired out or otherwise circulated in any form of binding or cover other than that in which
it is published. No part of this publication may be reproduced, stored in a retrieval system,
or transmitted in any form or by any means (electronic, mechanical, photocopying,
recording or otherwise) without the prior written permission of Nosy Crow Ltd.

A CIP catalogue record for this book is available from the British Library.

Printed in China

1 3 5 7 9 8 6 4 2

GUINEA PIG PARTY

Holly Surplice

nosy crow

10

Ten little guinea pigs,
dancing in a line.

Bump! Bump! go the guinea pigs,
and then there were . . .

Nine little guinea pigs think party games are great!

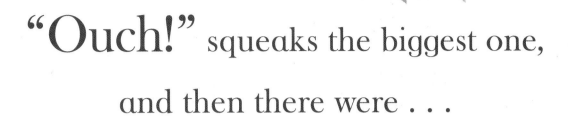

"Ouch!" squeaks the biggest one,

and then there were . . .

8 Eight little guinea pigs munch cake that tastes like heaven.

One gets greedy, eats too much,

and then there were . . .

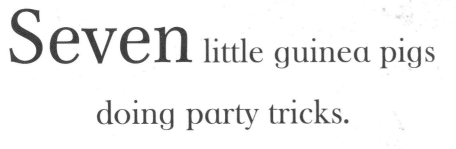

Seven little guinea pigs
doing party tricks.
Boing! Boing!
go the guinea pigs,
and then there were . . .

Six little guinea pigs

love to jump and dive!

One bumps his nose, and starts to cry,

and then there were . . .

 **Five** little guinea pigs pass the parcel on the floor.

One gets cross about her prize,

and then there were . . .

 **Four** little guinea pigs pop

balloons with glee!

One floats **up** and **up** with his,

and then there were . . .

3 Three little guinea pigs playing peek-a-boo.

One goes off to hide instead,

and then there were . . .

2

Two little guinea pigs
worn out from so much fun.

Bye-bye waves a guinea pig,

and then there was . . .

1

One little guinea pig

who wants to play again.

He shuts his eyes,

and makes a wish . . .

And once more there were . . .

ten!

10